# Henry's Tricks

by Donna Beveridge
illustrated by Brock Nicol

**Richard C. Owen Publishers, Inc.**
**Katonah, New York**

Holly took Henry to her friend's birthday party.

"Henry does tricks," she told everyone.

"Sit!" said Holly.

Henry sat.

"Shake!" said Holly.

Henry gave Holly his paw.

"Roll over!" said Holly.

Henry rolled over and over.

The children clapped and Henry wagged his tail.

"The next trick is fun," said Holly.

Holly put a dog biscuit on Henry's nose
and stepped back.

"Wait, Henry!" said Holly.

Henry sat very still and waited.

"Okay!" said Holly.

Henry flipped the biscuit into the air,
caught it in his mouth, and ate it.
The children laughed and Henry wagged his tail.

"You are a good dog, Henry!" said Holly.

Henry wiggled with joy.
He wiggled so hard he tipped the table,
and all the birthday presents slid to the floor.

"Oh, Henry! That's not a good trick," cried Holly.

Henry picked up the presents
one by one and carried them to Holly.

Everyone laughed and clapped.

"Oh, Henry," said Holly.
"That was your best trick!"